NICK JR The BACKYARDIGANS

A Merry Fair

by Jodie Shepherd
illustrated by The Artifact Group

SCHOLASTIC INC.
New York   Toronto   London   Auckland   Sydney
Mexico City   New Delhi   Hong Kong   Buenos Aires

Based on the TV series *Nick Jr. The Backyardigans*™ as seen on Nick Jr.®

No part of this publication may be reproduced, stored in a retrieval system, or transmitted in any form or by any means, electronic, mechanical, photocopying, recording, or otherwise, without written permission of the publisher. For information regarding permission, write to Simon Spotlight, an imprint of Simon & Schuster Children's Publishing Division, 1230 Avenue of the Americas, New York, NY 10020.

ISBN-13: 978-0-545-07599-2
ISBN-10: 0-545-07599-8

Copyright © 2008 by Viacom International Inc. All rights reserved. Published by Scholastic Inc., 557 Broadway, New York, NY 10012, by arrangement with Simon Spotlight, an imprint of Simon & Schuster Children's Publishing Division. NICK JR., *Nick Jr. The Backyardigans*, and all related titles, logos, and characters are trademarks of Viacom International Inc. NELVANA™ Nelvana Limited. CORUS™ Corus Entertainment Inc. READY-TO-READ is a registered trademark of Simon & Schuster, Inc. SCHOLASTIC and associated logos are trademarks and/or registered trademarks of Scholastic Inc.

12 11 10 9 8 7 6 5 4 3 2 1   8 9 10 11 12 13/0

Printed in the U.S.A.

First Scholastic printing, December 2008

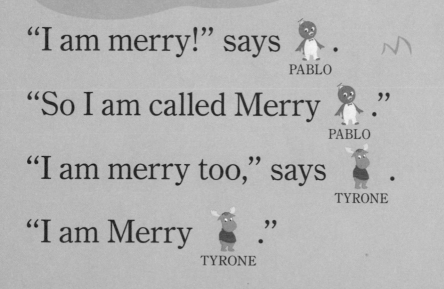

"I am merry!" says PABLO.

"So I am called Merry PABLO."

"I am merry too," says TYRONE.

"I am Merry TYRONE."

"I am also merry," says  ,
UNIQUA

"because today is the  fair."
CASTLE

"Princess  lives at the  ,"
TASHA CASTLE

says Merry  .
TYRONE

"She never smiles," says  .
PABLO

"We will go to the 🏰 fair
CASTLE

and make her smile," says 🫎 .
TYRONE

"Which way to the  ?"
CASTLE

asks  .
TYRONE

"I see nothing but  ."
TREES

"Oh, no!" cries  .
PABLO

"We are lost!

This is not merry at all."

So Merry  climbs on

UNIQUA

Merry 's shoulders.

PABLO

And Merry  climbs on

TYRONE

Merry 's shoulders.

UNIQUA

TYRONE can see the CASTLE

over the tops of the TREES .

"It is over there!" says TYRONE .

They go on their merry way.

"Halt!" a knight calls out.

It is Sir the Grumpy.

AUSTIN

"Who goes there?"

"We are two merry men," says PABLO .

"And one merry woman," says UNIQUA .

"We are going to the CASTLE

to make Princess TASHA merry too."

"Well, I am not merry,"
says Sir the Grumpy.

AUSTIN

"I am grumpy.

And you may not pass."

UNIQUA plays a merry tune.

PABLO and **TYRONE** dance a merry jig.

Soon Sir **AUSTIN** smiles.

"I feel merry now.

Just call me Sir **AUSTIN** the Merry."

"If we can turn

Sir  the Grumpy
AUSTIN

into Sir  the Merry,
AUSTIN

surely we can make

Princess  smile," says  .
TASHA   PABLO

They go on their merry way.

Finally they come to the  .

CASTLE

But the fair is not merry at all.

Princess is alone.
TASHA

She looks very sad.

UNIQUA dances around.

TYRONE and Sir AUSTIN leap and tumble.

Princess TASHA starts to smile.

Look!  is juggling.
PABLO

He juggles 4 at a time.
FOUR   TOMATOES

SMASH!

 needs more practice!
PABLO

But Princess TASHA looks merry.

"The TOMATOES made you smile!"

says PABLO.

"No," answers Princess TASHA.

"It was not the 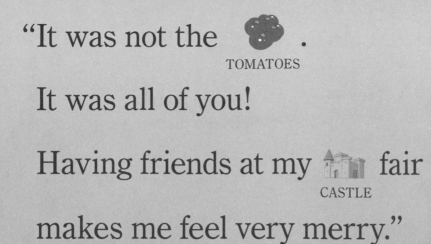.

It was all of you!

Having friends at my  fair

makes me feel very merry."

"We are three merry men,"

say Merry  ,  , and  .

PABLO   TYRONE   AUSTIN

"And we are two merry

women,"

add Merry  and .

UNIQUA   TASHA

"What a merry adventure!"

says .
TYRONE

"Those  made me hungry,"
TOMATOES

says .
PABLO

"Let's go to my  for a snack."
HOUSE